Mystery
on
October Road

Mystery on October Road

by
Alison Cragin Herzig
and
Jane Lawrence Mali

SCHOLASTIC INC.
New York Toronto London Auckland Sydney

ISBN 0-590-46011-0

12 11 10 9 8 7 6 5 4 3 2 1   2 3 4 5 6 7/9

Printed in the U.S.A.   28

First Scholastic printing, September 1992

*For Darrell and for
Bookends*

Chapter
· ONE ·

The minute I saw the two big hairy animals jump out of the van, I wanted to call Cats Cooney. But I wasn't sure she'd come, not after all the other times. Maybe she'd think I was stupid. I decided to call her anyway.

"You won't believe what's happening next door," I said. "There are these things, these animals."

"What animals? If the Bundys' cows have

gotten loose again, I'm not biking all the way over for that—"

"It's not the Bundys' cows. These things are bigger than cows."

"That's what you said about the bear in the tree that turned out to be a porcupine," Cats said. "And I've just gotten back from school. And I'm about to play touch football with my bro—"

"I can't talk anymore," I said. "Just come over. Please, please."

Up in my room, I edged the ruffled curtain to one side again. The van had been moved around to the back of the house. But the man in the big slouchy hat was gone. And so were the two whatever-they-weres. There was just the house with the sagging porch and the rusted mailbox and the big maple tree.

I wondered if Cats was going to bike over. She doesn't come to my house that often. October Road is too far away and too hilly and there's usually not that much to do. Nobody lives out here except us and the Bundys and they're really old. I'd been hoping a big family would move in. But the man and his hairy animals were better than nothing. Actually, they were the most interesting things that had happened, almost, since I was born.

I wished they'd come out again. But everything had gotten quiet. Except for the van it was as if I'd dreamed the whole thing up.

Where had they gone? Cats would be really mad if she came all the way out here for nothing.

I was still crouched by the window when the doorbell rang. "Why, Catherine," I heard Mom say. "I haven't seen you in ages."

"Hi, Mrs. Cooper."

I wished Mom had said Cats instead of Catherine, but maybe Cats hadn't noticed. Her feet pounded on the stairs. "This better be good, Casey," she yelled.

She was wearing her old green parka and her ponytail was frizzed out like a party snapper. Cats is the tallest, most popular girl in the fourth grade. I'm the shortest. Her hair is red and curly. Mine is brown and as straight as spaghetti. She has a lot of brothers. I don't have any. Other than that, we're exactly alike. Even our initials. She's Catherine Cooney and I'm Catherine Cooper. So we're both Catherines, only hardly anybody calls us that.

"I swear," Cats said, "if this is like when you said you'd seen Mrs. Briscoe's donkey with one leg totally missing. And you called the vet. And it turned out that his hoof was just caught in his halter . . ."

"Sssh," I said. "Here they come."

They were even bigger and hairier than the first time.

"They're dogs," Cats said after a minute.

My heart sank. "Only dogs?"

Cats squinted out the window. "Well, I think they're dogs. But they've got the longest legs I've ever seen and their tails hang down like elephant trunks. Maybe they're only part dog. Sort of part dog and part deer. Or part moose. But then they'd have antlers and their tails wouldn't be—"

"So aren't they great?" I asked.

The part-dogs galumphed around the van. Then one of them stood on its hind legs and peered through the windshield. The other one trotted onto the front porch. It reared up by the door.

"Look, it's ringing the doorbell," I said.

"They're taller than people," Cats said. "If it rings your doorbell, your mother will scream. I'm glad you called me. I'm glad you made me come over. Maybe they escaped from a zoo or . . ."

Then something even better happened and I grabbed Cats's arm.

The man had come out on the back steps. His slouchy hat was pulled way down over his eyes. And now he was tying a blue-and-white bandanna over his face, like a stick-up man in a Western movie.

Chapter
· **TWO** ·

The next day I was late for school. I slid into my seat just as Mrs. Briscoe was pulling the map down over the blackboard.

There was a note on my desk. "What happened after I left? What did he do? What about the dog things?" It was signed with a drawing of a really cute cat with frizzy whiskers.

I kept an eye on Mrs. Briscoe. "Mom says she thinks the dog things are Irish Wolfhounds," I wrote back. "They're part dog, part Irish, and part wolf." I signed it with a dog's head, but it turned out more like a pig.

"Catherines!" Mrs. Briscoe tapped the floor with her pointer.

"Tell you later," I whispered.

"This is England"—Mrs. Briscoe went back to her map—"where the Halloween tradition began. Ancient priests, called druids, believed that witches, demons, and ghouls roam the earth on the last day of October."

I sat up straighter. Halloween was a lot better than all the usual stuff about South America.

"The druids lit bonfires to scare off the bad spirits. If that didn't work, they tried to fool the spirits by dressing up like them. And they gave them good things to eat to make them happy."

"Candy corn!" everyone yelled. "Peanut-butter cups! Twizzlers! Chocolate kisses! Bubble gum!"

"That's enough," said Mrs. Briscoe.

"Did anything else happen?" Cats asked when the bell rang.

"He unloaded a lot of boxes," I said. "And parts of a bed and a rocking chair." I lowered my voice. "And something big and lumpy wrapped in a blanket." That's all I got to tell. Jennifer and Betsy pulled Cats away.

But after math I told her about the sounds in the night.

"Barking? Or screams?" Cats asked. "Or what?"

"Sort of like banging. And when I woke up this morning the front porch was fixed."

"What do you mean, 'fixed'?" Cats asked.

"It was all straight. There were new pieces of wood under the pillars and new front steps."

Cats always jumps rope with Jennifer and Betsy at recess. I'm not so good at jumping, but she's the best, even at double dutch. I waited until she was through.

"It's so weird," I said. "He wore that hat and the bandanna the whole time. Like he was hiding out or something."

"Maybe he's a spy. Or a bank robber," Cats said. "He's probably buried the money in the cellar and the police are after him." She sounded excited. "And the wolf dogs are trained to attack and—"

"I went over this morning to see if I could

pat them," I said. "But before I even got close, he called them back inside. He's not very friendly."

"Hey, Cats!" It was horrible Benny Dilmers. He sits right behind us in homeroom because his last name begins with D. "You want to go trick-or-treating with me on Halloween?"

"Beat it," Cats said. "I already promised Betsy and Jennifer."

I hadn't thought much about trick-or-treating. Usually I just go in the car with Mom.

"I'm going to wear a white sheet and a yellow hat," Benny said. "And go as a fried egg."

I almost laughed. I couldn't help it.

"So you could go as a sausage," Benny said.

Cats put up her fists. "I'm going to get you, Benny Dilmers," she yelled. Benny turned and ran. Cats tore across the playground after him. She's a fast runner and she caught him before he reached the swings. She says he's a geek, but sometimes I think she really likes him.

After school Cats said, "I want to see the weird man again."

"You do? Great!" It was neat to have Cats to

bike home with. "I wish we could think of some excuse to ring his doorbell," I said as we coasted down the last hill.

"We could offer to rake his lawn," Cats said, "or just stand under his window and yell 'fire' and he'd come barrelling out of there and—"

"And order the dogs to eat us," I said. "And we'd have to run for our lives."

When we got to my house, the whole downstairs smelled warm and doughy. Mom was in the kitchen wearing an apron over her blue jeans. She smiled when she saw Cats and gave us slices of bread with butter melting on them.

There were four more loaves lined up on the counter. Mom put two of them on a tray and covered them with a blue-and-white checked dish towel. "I made extra," she said. "I thought I might run them over to our new neighbor."

Cats and I stared at each other. "We'll do it," we said practically together.

Chapter
· THREE ·

"I'll ring the doorbell," Cats said. "You carry the tray."

But at the old rusted mailbox, she changed her mind. "Maybe you should ring the door-bell," she said. "It's your mother's bread."

The front walk was covered with brown and yellow leaves. They rustled and crunched under my feet.

"I always forget how loud leaves are," Cats said.

"Maybe he'll hear us coming and I won't have to ring," I said.

Cats followed me up the new steps onto the porch. "Casey, what if he really *does* sic the dogs on us? What if he has a gun? What if—"

"There's no doorbell," I said.

"You'll have to knock," Cats said.

I knocked and waited. No one answered. I knocked again, much louder.

"I guess he's not home."

"But the van's there," Cats said. "Try the window."

At first I couldn't see anything. And then—

"Something's moving," I whispered.

"Is it him?"

I shielded my eyes with my hands and pressed closer to the glass. The window looked into a small room. It was totally empty except for a rocking chair right in the middle of the bare floor. I jumped back.

"Did he see you?" Cats squealed.

"The chair," I whispered. "It's rocking. All by itself."

"What chair? What do you mean? What are you doing now?"

"You were right," I said. "He's there. I'm going to knock again."

"I'll check the other window," Cats whispered.

I was about to bang on the door when Cats screamed and dropped the tray. "Run, Casey!" The loaves of bread tumbled across the porch. "Run! He's looking right at me!"

I leapt down the steps after her. We tore back to my house and dove into the big pile of leaves at the end of the driveway.

"Eight feet tall!" Cats gasped. "And totally hairy."

"Was he wearing that hat? And the bandanna?"

"No. I could see his teeth and his tongue drooling out of his mouth! I swear, he's a monster or a werewolf."

"You sure it was him? Maybe it was one of those dogs?"

"Sure I'm sure," Cats said. Her ponytail was stuck with leaves. "I saw him clear as anything. I mean he was standing up just like a person."

"You want to go back? And see?" I asked.

"It's getting dark. I've got to get home."

"Come on. Please. I'll bet Mom would let you stay for supper."

"I know what," Cats said. "You watch him like anything and then we can meet at my old clubhouse tomorrow."

"I didn't know you had a clubhouse."

"I'll show you. After school."

I stood on the lawn for a while after she left, wondering about her clubhouse.

It was really quiet again. Lights came on in the kitchen. Dad was home from his job building houses. I could see him and Mom moving around inside. What would I tell her about the bread?

I had to go back.

I crept up the steps of the porch. One of the loaves was under a window. The other was by the railing. I wiped them on my jeans. Then I covered them with the dish towel and put the tray carefully down in front of the door.

That's when I heard a sound like panting from inside the house. And then a cough.

The porch boards creaked under my feet. I held my breath.

"Go away," a strange, hoarse voice said from right behind the door. "Leave me alone."

Chapter
· FOUR ·

The clubhouse turned out to be an old maple sugaring shack in the woods behind Cats's house. A sign that read THE C-PLUS CLUB was nailed to the door and someone had written KEEP OUT in white paint below it. The paint was peeling and the sign hung crooked.

Inside, a circle of upturned sap buckets surrounded a table made of boards and crates.

"Gee, this is a neat place," I said.

"My brothers and I used to come here a lot," Cats said. "The C is for Cooneys. Get it?"

"Hey," I said. "I'm a C, too."

Cats sat down on one of the buckets. I picked the one next to her. "So, what happened after I left?" she asked. A beat-up pack of cards lay on the table.

I told her about the voice through the door.

"He's definitely creepy." Cats hunched forward. "He's probably worse than a robber. One of those old ghouls. I'll bet he makes his next move on Halloween like Mrs. Briscoe said. And you live on October Road and—"

"There was a light on all last night," I said. "In his cellar. I saw it through the little window."

"The cellar? Benny's right. He said we ought to call the police."

"Benny? You didn't tell Benny Dilmers?"

"He knows stuff," Cats said. "And, besides, he's got this great pair of binoculars."

"I thought it was going to be just us."

"But, Casey? We could really use binoculars. We could see a lot better from your house."

"But he wants to call the police and tell every-body."

"We'll make him swear. He's really not that bad, Casey. I'm going to call him."

It didn't take Benny Dilmers more than three minutes to get to Cats's house. It was as if he'd been roosting on a telephone pole right down the road.

And he was loaded with stuff—the binoculars, some rope, a pair of handcuffs, his Boy Scout knife, and a pen that was also a flashlight.

"I'll bet he's a gangster," Benny said. He plopped down on an empty bucket right next to Cats. "I've read all about people like him. They come into a town and take over."

"Take over what?" I said.

"Everything. The hardware store, the police, the school—"

"I wouldn't mind if he took over school," said Cats.

"—I'll bet his whole cellar is full of guns."

"I was just thinking that." Cats was nodding her head like mad.

"But Cats, he didn't sound that mean."

"So we'll have to get in there first thing," Benny went on.

"Well," I said. "I guess it would be okay to watch him. So Cats, why don't you and I take the binoculars and go back to my house. Then we can spy on him after supper."

"But what about me?" Benny said. "My dad says these binoculars cost a lot of money. I have to be really careful with them."

His plaid shirt was buttoned crooked. It always was.

"We'll be careful," I said.

"But what if you have to wrestle him down?" Benny said. "Or handcuff him? You'll need at least three people for that."

"He's right," Cats said. "And remember the dogs, Casey."

"We may have to dig a tunnel under his lawn to get to his basement," Benny said. "I've read all about how to do that, too."

"Dig a whole tunnel?" I asked.

"That's a good idea," said Cats.

No it wasn't. It was stupid. Benny was a big mistake.

"Tomorrow's Saturday, so we can meet first thing," Benny said.

"Okay, Casey?" Cats asked. "At your house?"

"I guess," I said. It was better when it was just Cats and me.

I got on my bike to leave. Benny was still in the clubhouse. He was showing her how to work his flashlight pen.

By the time I wheeled onto October Road, it was getting dark. I almost missed the red flag on my mailbox. It was up. That was strange. Mom always picked up the mail in the morning.

But it wasn't mail. It was Mom's tray. And the dish towel. Then, way in the back, I saw a paper bag. For a moment I didn't want to reach in and touch it. It might be something dangerous, like a time bomb.

But I couldn't hear any ticking. And why would he blow up our mailbox anyway? I finally pulled the bag out with the tips of my fingers and peeked inside. It was full of apples and tangerines and nuts.

Chapter
· FIVE ·

"That was nice of him," Mom said. She emptied the paper bag into a wooden bowl.

"His name is John Smith," Dad said. "I heard that at the post office."

"Did you see him?" I asked.

"Nobody's seen him," Mom said.

Dad sat down at the kitchen table. "Where's the nutcracker?"

Mom handed him a hammer.

Now I had a lot to tell Cats. I ran to call her.

"John Smith!" Cats shouted into the phone. "I swear, nobody's named John Smith. He made that up."

"And he left a whole bag of food in our mailbox."

"Food? What kind of food?"

"Only apples and . . ."

"Apples. Wait. Benny says apples are the worst."

"Is Benny still there?" I asked.

"He says they're definitely poisoned, probably."

I could hear Benny yelling "don't touch them" in the background. "Do you really think so?" I said. "Then I'd better warn Mom and Dad."

But I was too late. There was a pile of shells and an apple core on the kitchen table in front of Dad. Mom stood by the sink finishing off a tangerine.

All through supper I kept waiting for one of them to keel over or throw up. But they didn't. By dessert I decided that maybe just some of the fruit was poisoned. But I had to get rid of the stuff that was left. I couldn't put it in the garbage. Mom would find it. So when I went to clear the table, I dumped the whole bowl into the clothes dryer.

Then later in my room I had a worse thought. What if it was a slow-acting poison? I opened my door so I could hear them in case they yelled for help. But all they did was argue about what had happened to the fruit and nuts. Finally they came upstairs to kiss me good night.

"How are you feeling?" I asked.

"A little gassy, thank you," Dad said. Mom was peering around my room.

"By the way, Casey, what are you wearing for trick-or-treating?" Dad asked.

"I haven't decided yet," I said.

"Maybe you could go with your friend Catherine this year," Mom said.

"She's going with Jennifer and Betsy. Or she may go as a fat sausage."

"A sausage?" Mom checked the top of my bureau and opened the closet door. "But she's so skinny."

"It's someone else's dumb idea."

"Did you bring the fruit upstairs, by any chance?" Mom asked.

"I wish it were a real family that moved in next door," I said.

After they left I got out of bed. The light was on in the man's cellar again. His whole house was dark except for that one little window close to the ground. I didn't know why, but it made me feel sad.

Maybe that fruit wasn't poisoned after all. Maybe that man, John Smith, wasn't a dangerous person with guns in his cellar, like Benny said. Maybe he was more like a druid. Druids gave food away. I wondered if they had big hairy dogs. Mrs. Briscoe hadn't said anything about that.

I went back to bed. Shadows moved across my ceiling. After a while, I heard Mom and Dad go into their room and close the door. The house grew quiet. Then all of a sudden I heard a noise from somewhere outside. *Scrape, scrape, scrape.* Stop.

I sat up and listened.

Scrape, scrape, scrape. Stop again. I crept to the window.

A half moon hung above the pine trees. The

dogs were out. I saw them right away. Their long shapes raced like black ghosts around the house. Then I saw the man in his slouchy hat. He was raking in the moonlight. *Scrape, scrape, scrape* toward a dark pile of leaves in the middle of his lawn.

Chapter
· SIX ·

Cats arrived the next morning before I'd finished my breakfast.

"Where are your parents?" she asked first thing. "Did they, uh, you know, get sick last night?"

"They've gone to the garden center. Hey, I'm glad you didn't bring Benny."

"Well, actually"—Cats looked toward the window—"he's outside. Digging."

I carried my orange juice glass to the sink.

Then I opened the dryer door and piled the fruit and nuts back into the bowl. "I don't think this stuff is poisoned," I said. "Want an apple?"

"No way," Cats said.

"Okay. I'll give it to Benny."

Benny was under the pine trees with a long-handled shovel. "Have an apple," I said.

"Gee, thanks." He took a big bite and handed me the shovel. "You keep digging. I'm going to climb this pine tree and take a look through my binoculars."

I dug a few shovelfuls of dirt. Then I stopped. "This is stupid," I whispered to Cats. Benny was grunting and scraping around in the branches above my head. "A tunnel will take us years."

"I was just going to say that," said Cats.

There was a gasp from Benny and a shower of pine needles. Then a half-eaten apple fell out of the tree. I looked up. Benny was scrambling down as fast as he could with the binoculars swinging from his neck.

"I saw him," he said even before he reached the ground. "Through the window. Dressed for Halloween. Already."

"In a costume?" Cats said.

"Like a big bunny suit?" I asked.

"Not a costume. Just a mask. Like something out of a horror movie. And he's wearing a stocking over his head so he looks like he has no hair."

"Maybe he's just bald," I said.

"He's hairy," Cats said. "I know."

"It was a stocking," Benny insisted. "I could see."

"Do you think he's crazy?" Cats asked.

"Are you crazy?" Benny said. "Of course he's crazy."

"Ssh!" I said. "I hear something."

Cats peered over my shoulder.

"It's the van," I said. "He's leaving."

"Hit the dirt," Benny said. "He'll see you."

"So what? I live here," I said. "Besides, I want to see him."

The van backed out of the driveway. I only got a quick look through the side window as it went past my house. He was wearing his same slouchy hat and the blue bandanna over his nose.

"Get up!" I said to Benny. "There's no mask."

"There is too. It had a screaming mouth and no ears."

"I don't believe you."

"He probably pulled it off and left it in the cellar with all the other stuff."

"Maybe Benny's right," Cats said. "I mean, *he* had the binoculars."

The sound of the van faded into the distance.

"If I could get in there, I could prove it," Benny said.

"He's gone," Cats said. "So why can't we just go over, like we're visiting or something?"

"Okay, but I still say there's no mask," I said.

Benny led the way with his binoculars and the shovel and his notebook and his dumb flashlight pen.

We sneaked around the house. All the doors were locked and there were new-looking shades over most of the windows.

"I wish I had a wire hanger," Benny said. "I've read all about how to pick locks."

"Wait, Casey!" Cats whispered. "Look over there."

A whole row of bulging black garbage bags leaned against the far side of the house.

"Don't touch them," Benny said. "They're probably full of explosives."

Cats giggled nervously. "Maybe he's planning to blow up the whole town."

I hesitated. Nobody left explosives out in plain sight. Besides, I wanted to prove what a dummy Benny was. "Give me the shovel," I said.

"What are you going to do?" Cats asked.

I poked one of the bags with the tip of the shovel. Something rustled.

"Watch out!" Benny yelled.

"It's only leaves," I said. I opened the bag to show him. "See. Leaves. Told you he was raking."

"You never know," Benny muttered.

I didn't answer. I was looking at something else. Behind the bag was another small narrow window. Like the cellar window I could see from my room. But this one was propped open.

Chapter
· SEVEN ·

"You're not going to try to squeeze through there?" Cats said. "I swear it'll be dark and full of spiders and snakes and you don't know how far the floor is so you could just drop and drop until you broke your leg and then—"

"I've got my penlight," Benny said, "so I guess I should go first."

I didn't want Cats to think he was braver than me. "I found the window."

"Okay," Benny said. "I'll go second."

Cats still looked worried. "But that's breaking and entering."

"No, it isn't," Benny said. "It's only entering."

He lifted the window all the way up. I slid through on my stomach, legs first. For a moment I hung there, feeling around with my feet. Nothing. Benny held the little light as far in as he could. It didn't help much. I still couldn't see the floor. What if Cats was right? What if I dropped into an old well?

I took a deep breath and let go.

My feet hit hard floor. I was so surprised I sat down.

"Are you okay?" Above me I could see Benny's face in the open square of window.

"No problem," I said. But even with the window, it was pretty dark down there. And it smelled damp and moldy. Benny squished himself through the opening. Cats dropped after him.

Benny swung his penlight around. The little yellow circle landed on a stool and then a workbench next to the wall. It stopped on a box at the foot of some stairs.

"What did I tell you?" Benny said. "Bet you the mask is in there."

Cats held onto my jacket and I stuck close to Benny. He shone the light on the top of the box. It glinted off a piece of metal set in the wood. "It's a name plate." I bent over. "And it's got John Smith on it," I said.

"He's probably put John Smith on everything," Benny said. "To cover his tracks. Go ahead. Open her up."

I kept looking at the name plate. It looked old, like it had been there forever. Suddenly I didn't want to open the box.

"Okay, I'll do it," Benny said. He undid the two hooks and raised the lid.

"It's all knives," Cats whispered. "And mallets and gougers and torture stuff and . . . "

"Those aren't knives," I said. "They're mostly chisels. Dad uses them to make shelves for Mom." Each of the chisels had their own slot and they were lined up according to size.

Benny swung the light away. "That mask must be somewhere," he said.

"Wait. I've got to close this box. Leave it like it was."

"What's that?" asked Cats. "Over there in the corner."

I slipped the little hooks back into their catches. "I think we ought to get out of here," I said. All of a sudden I didn't want to be in his cellar poking through his things anymore. "I mean, he could come back any minute."

"Not yet," Benny said. "Cats has found something really big."

He shone his light on the something. It was covered with an old blanket.

"Maybe we should leave it," I said.

"Don't be a chicken," Benny said. "When I count three we'll all pull the blanket off together. Okay? One, two, three."

"A head!" Cats screamed. "A cut-off head!"

Benny dropped the flashlight. He scrambled toward the window.

Cats ran after him. "It's a horse. And it's dead."

"Wait!" At my feet Benny's light was still shining. The horse's red mouth gaped open. Its ears were flattened back. "No, it isn't. It's okay."

But Cats was trying to reach the windowsill. Benny dragged the stool over and climbed up.

"It's only wood," I yelled at them.

I saw Benny's feet kick through the opening. Cats was right behind him.

"Hurry up, Casey," Cats shouted.

I was still holding the blanket. I didn't know what to do with it.

"Quick!" I could see Benny's legs jumping up and down outside. "The van's coming!"

I threw the blanket at the horse and ran. The stool teetered underneath me. I made a grab for the window ledge. Then the stool keeled over and I crashed with it.

Chapter
· EIGHT ·

For a moment I lay on the cellar floor with the stool on top of me.

"Casey! You've got to get out of there." It was Cats. Her head and shoulders stuck through the window. "Here, grab my hand." She reached an arm down.

I tried to get up. But there was something wrong with my ankle.

Then I heard barking and whining and the

scratch of claws on the door at the top of the stairs. They were coming!

Cats's arm disappeared. I was all alone. And there was no place to hide. Except under the work bench. Or the blanket. Maybe I could crawl. But I was too scared to decide.

And it was too late. The door opened and the huge wolf dogs came charging down the stairs.

I covered my head with my arms and closed my eyes. I waited for the dogs to bite me.

"Down, Tartan! Wolf!" ordered the man's hoarse voice.

Nothing happened. I opened my eyes a crack. The dogs were lying flat on the floor, their big hairy heads inches from my feet. I scrunched back against the wall, as far away from them as I could get.

A light bulb in the ceiling went on and the man loomed over me in his hat and bandanna. My heart was beating so hard I could hardly breathe.

The man didn't say anything. He just stood staring at me like I was a bug or something. I ducked my head again. Then I saw his feet step over my legs and I heard the cellar window close with a bang.

Now I was really trapped. And my ankle hurt. I wanted to cry.

The dogs whined and edged closer. One of them sniffed my bad foot. I drew my legs up and hugged my knees.

The man bent over his tool chest. I saw him take out the chisels, one by one, as if he were counting them. Finally he closed the lid and came back toward me. I felt like throwing up. What was he going to do? He picked up the stool and set it back by the work bench. Then he shook out the blanket and covered the horse's head again.

Where were Cats and Benny? Maybe they'd gone to get help.

"So what did you take?" the man demanded suddenly. His voice made me jump.

"Nothing," I whispered. The word didn't come out. "Nothing," I repeated.

"Then what in blazes are you doing down here?"

"I'm sorry," I said. I swallowed to get the lump out of my throat. "I'm really sorry. But . . . but . . . we thought you were hiding. We thought you had guns . . ."

"Guns!"

"And Benny said you wore a mask." Now that I'd started I couldn't stop. "And I said you didn't, but he said he could prove it . . ."

"So that's it." The man made a hoarse sound from behind the bandanna. "I should have known."

I held my breath. My ankle hurt every time I moved my toes.

One of the dogs whimpered. The man reached down and patted its head. The dog licked his hand. Somehow that made me feel a little better. "So you want to know if I wear a mask," he said in his scary voice. "You and everyone else."

"No . . ."

But before I could tell him it was okay, he yanked the bandanna down and pulled off his hat. "Well, see for yourself."

For a moment I thought Benny was right. The

man's mouth was just a dark hole in his face and the skin all around it was stretched tight. One of his ears was shaped funny. And there was no hair on that side of his head.

But it wasn't a mask. It was his real face.

"If you're thinking about screaming, don't. You'll scare the dogs."

I couldn't stop staring. I wondered if it hurt him to talk.

"Are you through?" the man asked. "Have you seen enough?"

I nodded.

"Then get up and get out of here." The man jammed his hat back on his head.

He was letting me go. I didn't care how much my ankle hurt. If I couldn't walk, I'd hop.

"Now what's wrong with you?" the man demanded.

I hopped faster. "Nothing."

"You always walk like a pogo stick?" He didn't sound as angry as before.

"I'm okay, really." The dogs were still lying down, but they were watching me. Three more hops, I told myself, and I'd be past them.

"Wait," the man said. I was almost at the stairs. "Did you hurt yourself?"

"I can make it."

But he put a hand under my elbow and snapped his fingers. The dogs rose to their feet and followed us slowly up the steps.

Chapter
· NINE ·

I thought the man was going to lead me right out the door. But when we reached the kitchen he made me sit down at the table. "It only hurts a little," I said. "It'll be fine as soon as I get home." I curled my other foot around the leg of the chair.

He took off my sneaker, anyway, and my sock, and pressed his fingers gently all around my ankle.

"Ouch!"

"Sorry," he said. "But it's not broken. It's only a sprain. Stay here." His mouth made Os when he talked and his skin looked shiny, like pulled taffy. But he had a regular nose and regular eyes. "I'm going to get some tape," he added.

One of the dogs rested its chin on my shoulder. The other one sniffed my neck.

"Do your dogs bite?" I asked. I didn't want to be left alone with them.

"They're big babies." He smiled, sort of. It was a lopsided smile, but it made his face look almost nice.

While he was gone, the dogs kept nudging at my hands. Finally I tried patting them a little. Their long curved tails waved, so I scratched behind their ears. They liked that even more. They wouldn't let me stop. It was like a game.

"What's that horse in your cellar?" I blurted out when the man came back.

"I made it." He knelt by my bad foot.

"Is that why you have all those chisels?"

He began to wrap a stretchy bandage around my ankle. "I used to carve animals for carousels," he said after a minute.

"That horse is so good. I mean, people scream when they see it."

"People scream at a lot of things." He stopped wrapping and pulled the bandanna up over his mouth and his crumpled ear.

"That's because it looks so real," I said.

The man shook his head. "I don't do it anymore." He sounded angry again, but I'd stopped being scared.

"But why? You're a really great carver."

"Doesn't matter," the man said. "The fire fixed that. Burned everything. Everything," he repeated in a low voice. Then he fastened the bandage with two metal clips and handed me my sock. "There. That should feel better." Above the bandanna his eyes were dark brown.

"The fire . . ." I hesitated. "Is that what happened to your face?"

"I was a fool. I went back in to get my tools." He finished lacing up my sneaker. "See if you can walk on that ankle."

I limped around the table. The tight bandage made it a lot easier. One of the dogs walked beside me, like it wanted to help. "Good boy,

Tartan," the man said. "Now let's get her home."

I sort of wanted to stay in the kitchen a little longer, but the man opened the back door. We all trooped out on the porch. Wolf galloped around us. But Tartan stuck with me. He was almost as tall as I was.

"Is your name really Mr. John Smith?" I asked, as we crossed his lawn.

"Yes, believe it or not." His eyes crinkled up. I figured that behind the bandanna he was smiling his weird one-sided grin.

Then I spotted two shapes crouched under the pine trees. Benny and Cats! I'd forgotten about them. Cats had a hand up to her mouth, like she was about to scream, and Benny's face was one big pair of binoculars. He had them trained right on us.

"You can go back now, Mr. Smith," I said. "I mean, I can make it okay from here. Really."

I didn't want him to see them staring.

Chapter
· TEN ·

"So he's not a spy or a ghoul at all," I said. Cats sat on the bed with me. Benny wandered around my room looking at things. "He's more like a, what Mrs. Briscoe said, a druid."

"I want to meet him." Cats hugged my pillow. "I've never met someone who got burned. I've never met someone with a funny ear, I've—"

"I want to meet him, too," Benny interrupted. "See him up close."

"Take us over, Casey. Okay?" Cats added. "Now that you know him."

"Maybe tomorrow," I said. I wondered if my ankle was all black and blue under the bandage.

"What's wrong with now?" Benny shuffled through the papers on my desk.

"I've just been there," I said.

"So it's our turn," said Benny.

"I don't think he likes people looking at him." I tested my foot on the floor. "Besides, my ankle hurts."

"You were walking on it okay before. I saw you." Benny leaned over to peer at my math homework. His binoculars bumped against my desk.

"Please, Casey," Cats begged. "It'll be fun."

My ankle didn't hurt that bad. Maybe Mr. Smith wouldn't mind. And if the dogs liked Cats too, she might come out to my house a lot more.

"I want to see his mouth," Benny said. "Hey, I want to see if he can whistle." He put his binoculars up to his eyes and peered at me through the wrong end.

I remembered Mr. Smith's one-sided smile.

"No," I said. "I don't want to."

Benny lowered the binoculars and glared at me. "Why not?"

"Because I just don't!"

"Then I'll go by myself. You want to come, Cats?"

"I don't know. Maybe. I guess," Cats said. "Okay, Casey?"

I didn't say anything. Benny turned at the door. "And besides, you got the third math problem wrong," he said. "It's not twelve eggs."

I watched from my window. Cats and Benny argued for a while at the edge of Mr. Smith's lawn. Then Benny started up the walk, but he only went halfway. Cats waited by the mailbox. Finally they got on their bikes and rode away.

Now there was all of Saturday left. And nothing to do.

I wondered how I was going to ride my bike. I couldn't even walk around my room without limping. And Mom would notice. I wondered if Mr. Smith was going to tell on me.

Maybe I should write him a really sorry note, saying I'd never do it again. And please, please don't tell my parents.

"Casey? You there?" Dad called from downstairs. They were home.

Right away Mom said, "Are you limping?"

"No. I just twisted my ankle a little."

"You feel like carving pumpkins?" Dad asked. "We got the three best at the garden center."

That cheered me up. "I want the one with bumps," I said.

"All I want are the seeds," Mom licked her lips. "When you roast them with a little olive oil and salt, they're delicious."

Dad carried the pumpkins into the kitchen.

"Good heavens!" Mom stared at the table. "I must be losing my mind. There's that fruit. Back again."

I picked up the bowl really quickly and put it on the counter. Dad covered the table with newspaper. In Mom's utensil drawer the spoons and scrapers and stuff were in separate compartments and the knives were lined up according to size. Like Mr. Smith's chisels.

"Hey, slowpoke," Dad said. "We're all ready to go here."

Dad carved lots of teeth. He always does that. I did circle eyes and a triangle nose and a smiley mouth. It looked kind of boring. So I made whiskers. The whiskers turned it into a cat's face.

When I was through, I took my pumpkin upstairs. Maybe I'd give it to Cats on Monday.

Then I had a better idea. I got out my note paper with the little umbrella in the corner. First I wrote the very sorry, never, never again part. After that I wrote the part about please, please don't tell. I signed it "The girl who didn't take anything, Casey Cooper." Then I added a P.S. "This is for you for Halloween. I carved it myself. It's supposed to be a cat in case you can't tell, like you carved your horse. If you ever need someone to dogsit, I can watch them and feed them and play with them. I think Tartan really likes me. Your friend, Casey Cooper."

I sealed the note, picked up the pumpkin, and got my jacket. Then I sort of hop-walked over to Mr. Smith's house. I left the pumpkin right outside the back door where he'd be sure to find it.

Chapter
· ELEVEN ·

I sort of hoped Mr. Smith would write back, but he didn't. And the van was gone when I woke up on Sunday. Then, when I looked again, it was parked right next to his kitchen door. But I didn't see him. I only saw the dogs when he let them out to run. I could tell them apart now. Tartan was taller and a little grayer. Wolf was the one who galloped around in circles.

By Sunday night my ankle was worse. I took off the bandage and ran cold water on it in the tub. But nothing helped. Finally I had to tell Mom.

She drove me to the doctor first thing Monday morning and then to school. Mrs. Briscoe stopped the whole class when I came through the door on crutches. "Why, Catherine," she said, "whatever happened to you?"

"I sprained my ankle," I said. "I have to stay off it until the swelling goes down."

Cats stared at me. Benny stared at my crutches.

"We were waiting and waiting for you," Cats said the moment the bell rang.

"Did he tell your parents?" Benny asked. "About us, I mean."

I shook my head. "But the light doesn't go on in the cellar anymore. Only in the kitchen."

"You see, Benny Dilmers?" Cats said. "I swear, I told you he was probably nice and Casey was right and she was really brave and . . ."

Brave? Nobody'd ever called me brave before.

"Then I'm going to go out there. On Halloween," Benny said. "I'm going to ring his door-bell. And I've had crutches, too. I know all about them. I even know how to do stairs." He stomped off.

Cats carried my books down the hall. "Does it hurt?" she asked. "Can you still go trick-or-treating on Wednesday?"

"I guess so. Mom's going to drive me around."

"No. I mean with us. Me and Betsy and Jennifer. I already told them."

That made me feel really good. "Okay," I said. "But I haven't decided about my costume."

"I'm going as a baseball player. My brothers have all these old uniforms at home. And Betsy's going as a witch and Jennifer is going as her broom and . . ."

"You're really lucky to have brothers," I said.

By the time I got to school on Wednesday I'd almost decided to cover myself with bandaids and pretend I was a wounded soldier. But then Cats pulled a baseball uniform out of her book-bag. "Here's another one," she explained. "My brothers said you can go as a player on the dis-abled list."

"Is it the same as yours?" I asked.

"Yes," Cats said. "I swear, we'll be exactly alike, except for your crutches."

That night Mom offered to drive everyone. She sat in front all by herself. Me and Cats and Jennifer and Betsy all squished into the back seat. Cats said it was more fun that way. And at all the houses, when the people opened the door, she said, "The crutches are real," and pointed at me. "Her whole leg is swollen and mashed and sprained . . ." So everyone gave me extra candy. Even Mrs. Briscoe. She gave me two caramel apples. I gave both of them to Mom. No one else wanted them. By the time we were through, Cats had to carry my trick-or-treat bag. It was so heavy it clunked.

"Okay, girls," Mom said finally. "That's enough candy to last you a year."

She dropped Jennifer and Betsy off first.

"Bring your bag to school tomorrow," Cats said before she got out of the car. "We'll make trades."

I got into the front seat with Mom.

"Did you have a good time?" she asked.

I nodded. It was my best Halloween ever. But it was nice to be going home.

October Road was dark and quiet. The moon was a little sliver above the outline of the trees. A rabbit hopped in front of us at the top of the last hill. Mom slowed the car.

"Good heavens," she said suddenly. "What's that?"

I peered through the windshield. Beyond our house at the bottom of the hill there was a strange glow, like fire in the grass.

Mom pulled into our driveway.

That's when I saw all the jack-o'-lanterns in front of Mr. Smith's house. Everywhere. All carved. And all lit up.

I forgot my candy. I forgot to close the car door. It was like nothing I'd ever seen before. So many yellowy orange faces glowing in the dark.

Mom ran after me with my crutches. "I don't believe this," she said. "I've got to get your father. I've got to call everybody."

Jack-o'-lanterns circled Mr. Smith's mailbox. They lined his walk. And the porch steps. There was a devil with flame eyes and a cannibal with a bone through its nose and a Humpty Dumpty with a carved bowtie and high collar. And a lion and a rat and an owl. At the end of the walk was a big fat Buddha. Its whole head was covered with tight little curls. I could see candlelight shining through them. And on the porch steps was a monster with snaggle teeth and horns that really stuck up.

They were all so different.

I wanted to stop. I wanted to go back. But there were more.

On the railing was a Pocahontas and a sad clown with tears on his cheeks. And three little pigs all together. And a ghost. The ghost looked just like a ghost. Its whole head glowed in the dark, from the inside out.

How did Mr. Smith do that? I bent closer. Almost all the orange pumpkin skin had been peeled off. He'd only left it where he wanted dark circles for the eyes and an O for the mouth.

"Casey!" It was Dad. "You've got to come over here. And see."

"Wait." I hadn't even finished with the peeled ghost and I needed to check the others again.

"It's too wonderful," Mom called. I limped down the porch steps. The Pocahontas had a carved Indian headband I hadn't even noticed before.

Dad pointed toward the pine trees. His other arm was around Mom.

Under the pine trees was a jack-o'-lantern all by itself. With a girl's face.

I stared and stared.

It was me. He'd carved a pumpkin with hair as straight as spaghetti.

It was better than a note. It was better than anything.

I wanted to go and knock on his door and tell him. But then I heard a car door slam and the Bundys' voices. And there were more cars coming, headlights on the road. I'd have to wait until tomorrow.

I looked back at Mr. Smith's house, wondering if he was in there, watching from behind the shades. That's when I saw the very last pumpkin. In the dark window of his kitchen was the cat's face I'd carved, lit up and grinning out at me.